EMBRACE

RAGHAVI JHANJEE

An Imprint of

MAPLE PRESS PRIVATE LIMITED
office: A 63, Sector 58, Noida 201 301, U.P., India
phone: +91 120 455 3581, 455 3583
email: info@maplepress.co.in
website: www.maplepress.co.in

Embrace *by* Raghavi Jhanjee

ISBN: 978-93-90292-46-2

10 9 8 7 6 5 4 3 2 1

Cover Design @ Umesh Semwa

Dedicated to

My Family and Friends

Contents

Acknowledgement

Getting here was arduous but worth it. I am thankful to my family and friends who stood by me, helped me and cheered me on. I would also like to thank my faculty at Bennett University for their guidance and support throughout.

I hope my words warm your hearts...

Cruising

Don't hold me back,
Let me run my course fair and square,
Let me stumble,
And be whole again.

1

Aversion to crowds crawled back in,
The words that once screeched confidence,
Chose to stay mum.
The whirl and world all hit at once,
And then the snake-skin shed.
Passers-by gave a knock,
Once, twice
While the exterior was wordless dumb,
The insides cried.
Mirrors are truth-bearers,
But I felt in that moment they lied
Just then the snake-skin shed yet again.

2

She didn't utter a single word,
But her eyes spoke in abundance.
I could tell those eyes were filled with sadness,
But no tear dropped from them.
It seemed the ocean had struck a drought,
The pain was making room in deadly silences.
The time didn't heal her,
It made her lifeless.
She had drifted far away,
From voices that gave her assurance that it will be alright.
Deep down she was sure,
Nothing will be the same.
Many came to light fires,
From her ashes,
But ashes never light up.
She was done hiding from the darkness,
So she made it a part of herself.

3

If only I had the wind in my wings,
I wouldn't feel heavy and aim higher.
My thoughts would soar,
All unleashed at one go.
My words are my prowess,
I word power, strength, fuel waves and turn tables.
Unstoppable, I push against the barriers set by you,
Bathe in confidence, my regrets are few.
You don't tell me where I belong,
I pave my paths, I strangle storms.
I prepare at dusk to rise at dawn,
My mind is but a silenced chaos.
It feels, it sees and it voices.
All at once,
Sometimes nothing at all.

4

Unwavered spirit, unfazed by failures,
A work in progress,
Rising above all odds.
Unapologetic in what I am,
Imperfections all proudly shone.
I adorn grace, strength and determination,
Falling down, dusting off and trying yet again.
The words that find it hard to make their way through my mouth,
Have learnt to flow through my ink.
All that I bottled up inside,
Is all what I want to set free.

5

That empty feeling in the pit of my stomach,
Expressionless face, lost in an unspoken quest,
A heavy heart with a crater like void.
Eyes following an endless gaze,
To know is always simpler,
Than to be caught in between.
A path makes more sense,
Than dwindling midway.
For when you find yourself overwhelmed,
Hold on,
Believe.
Because when it makes no sense,
It always falls into place.

6

You unearthed the wounds,
Inflicted by someone else.
Thought you were different,
But no! I was yet again digging my own grave.
All these years you stood by me,
Then seasons changed and so did you.
Look at you, you seem unaffected,
The master of the art of pretence,
The very shoulder that vanished my tears,
Gave me reasons to shed more.
I have toughened up now,
So don't knock at my door,
When you'll be left alone by the one you left me for,
You'll find me stone-cold, not caring anymore.

7

Who am I?
A clueless wanderer
Conjuring a mesh of thoughts
On my painted sky
Or am I the hand holding a little too tightly
Too afraid of letting go
Am I an ocean of feelings bottled up inside,
A string of fear, presenting a show of strength
I feel I am what I want to be,
Believing, breaking and believing yet again.

8

I know not the ending of the paths I take,
Or what I'll ace and what I'll fail.
But I follow the sound of my heartbeat,
Listening closely to its desire,
Supporting it in confusion and in clarity.
I know not the future,
In the present I dive deep.
There are times when I feel so helpless,
Adjusting to the highs and lows.

9

I considered myself,
A mere fragment in this vast world,
Questioning my worth, my purpose and my existence.
Growing up, the fog descends,
From my life's mirror.
And I see clearly,
Figuring out my worth,
Adding meaning to my being.

10

Treaded carefully all these years,
On the surface mostly,
Sceptical of falling in too deep.
Evolution helped me grow,
Falling in deeper,
Letting in the rush,
Something I've never felt before.
Letting it sink in, unafraid,
Ready to fall again.

11

Trying to thrive,
Midst the burden of lies,
People leading double lives.
Parasites feeding on goodness,
Taking in the little of what is left.
Broken souls crave for love,
Happy faces, empty inside.
Subdued in darkness,
Searching for the light.

12

Trapped in normalcy,
I crave for something more.
Something that fuels my zest for life,
Challenges my courage,
Endangers my happiness,
Piques my curiosity,
Crawls me towards the end,
And leaves me mid-air,
Where I'm not afraid to make choices,
Pushing through the darkness.
Where at one second I'm racing,
And in the next, the world stands still.

13

Coming in terms with myself,
I uncover my scars,
Illuminate the darkness inside.
My voice, raw
My face not one with many,
My silent demeanor,
Breaking out of meaningless talk.
Unruffled by opinions,
Refusing submission.

14

Broken vases can be fixed,
But their visible cracks,
Represent devastated core.
A thing of beauty,
Smiles through pain.
Climbing each day,
Striving to emerge from battles.
A cracked vase, crooked-edged,
With courage undeterred.

15

I looked forward at daybreak,
Vastness consumed me.
I let out a shout,
To check my significance,
Retreating after realizing its littleness.
Shadows building around,
Clouding my sight.
Dusting off, sprouting up,
Crawling, walking and running.

16

Pulling me down
Cutting my fingers
Suppressing my decibel
Tying my legs
Inflicting me with pain
Bandaging me till I am unable to see my scars
Brooding soul let out a struggling smile
Accompanied by an unheard sigh

17

A box I locked,
Stored away the younger me,
I wasn't proud of,
Felt so small,
Sometimes even nothing at all.
Tucked her in a deep sound sleep,
Yearning acceptance, didn't let her weep.
What the little me understood the hard way,
Applied it while growing up.
Consumed the harsh realities,
Instead of the little girl's fairytale.

18

We are faulty people,
Fitting in a seemingly perfect world.
Constantly being put under labels,
Scanned through perceptions.
Covering our tracks,
Hiding away the invalidations.
Altering our life story to fit in well,
Changing moulds,
Changing shapes.

19

As darkness unfurls,
The sounds grow quieter.
No hint of light,
The demons pry in the night.
A trickle down your forehead, a tinted smile,
That crooked look behind innocent eyes.
Intentions change,
Feelings dissolve.
The heart grows cold,
The body is numb.
Sinister flows midst the glistening glow,
A faceless war of words ensues.
It's all a game creeping behind shadows,
Colour fading into the deadly silent meadows.

20

You find yourself gazing out,
Clueless of your actions.
Unwavered by the surroundings,
Caving in to your thoughts.
Voices in your head,
Churning you to the core.
Finding your way back can take a while,
You can be pulled in deeper,
Or can move towards gradual escape.

21

I've looked for my voice,
In crowds and closed spaces.
Looked for relatability in people's words,
And comfort in fuzziest of hugs.
Been lost more than finding myself,
Was more doubtful than thoughtful.
Found solace in books,
Happiness in loneliness.
Yearning each day to fill that void,
Learning, hurting and growing.

Matters of the Heart

Hear the sound closely,
It has something to say
Open your soul,
Don't let the feelings run away.

22

A withered rose,
Cannot be breathed back to life.
A cold embrace,
Distances lovers further.
Shut my eyes,
Cradle me in your arms,
Tell me you're not lying,
When you think it's perfect.
When you say my eyes are so sublime,
Can't hold me for long,
You drift away.
Looking for a reason,
A way out.
When it's all a burden to you,
It's better to drift away,
Then to fallout.

23

I wish I could tell you about the chaos in my head,
I do miss it all,
But I guess now it's just too late.
Although I blame the time,
But it's me who is to be blamed.
I feel I let go of something,
I feel I made a mistake.
But then the thought of getting back,
Scares me to death,
What if I end up hurting you again?
Since I can't trust my mind,
The decisions it makes,
The paths it frequently changes.
I can't trust myself anymore.
The toxicity that you felt was mine,
It has always been mine.

24

People describe love as comfortable silence,
I've felt, it is but a drug,
Good while it lasts,
Wears off after a point of time.
The sand slips through the fingers,
Leaving tiny remnants.
A chance for you to sustain the essence,
Or let it fade away.
Till nothing is left,
Nothing, to stay.

25

I saw you smile at me after days,
The warmth radiated from your face.
You lie when you look away,
Can't stare at me,
Don't choose to stay.
You move forward,
She pulls you away.
I longed for you for such a long time,
Can't wait no more,
No tears left to cry.
Tired of your ways of lighting up my hopes,
And then running them dry.

26

You hold me close,

I feel your warm breathing on my ear.

Hands entwined,

Hearts adding music to silence.

Your hand makes its way to the small of my back,

The other finds its way to the strands of my hair.

And when your eyes meet mine,

Lost in a gaze so raw, so pure.

Emotions flow,

And we dive in deeper.

27

And here I am with my heart on my sleeve,

With a rocky past, a part of me,

But not defining my present.

'Cause it is the nature of how life functions,

You encounter, you fall, you get up and fall yet again.

Aren't we all bound to continue believing?

Our premise, our very essence thrives on belief.

I stopped writing for a while after you left,

My ink had developed a liking towards you, you see.

It would flow when you smiled or when you effortlessly gave in to your vulnerability.

It counted the heartbeats when you breathed closer till no space was left open,

And our bodies happily fused together.

It comforted your tears and kept you warm when I was not around.

But then those pages grew distant,

As if they no more craved to be written upon.

Drowning in voluntary seclusion,

Their binding no more strong, slowly falling apart.

When you finally walked out, there was a pause,

The hardest part you see is the sinking in.

When each part of me screamed to be touched one last time,

And the heart wanted to clutch on to the idea of you staying

for once.
It is all but a matter of time,
Before we fall again,
'Cause you see, we never stop
Rather go through a momentary pause.
Picking up our pieces and building piece by piece.
So today I stand with my heart wide open,
My pages not so distant,
My ink ready to believe again.

28

And all I wanted was him,
The idea still lingers of what we would be like.
His touch seems distant now,
His eyes don't wander often in my direction.
He seems to let go of me,
Though we've never been together.
Still our eyes meet to look away,
A constant struggle of finding words to say.
I wish I knew about love,
The concept is still not clear.
Not that I don't have those cold rushes,
Cliché dreamy eyes and impatience to meet.
It's just that I want you to take me to your depths,
Your fears, your vision and everything that caused you despair.
I feel I've lost something,
Even before I had it.

29

I wish I could write more,
But words left me,
After I left you.
The cracks refuse to repair,
Allowing pain to seep in.
Didn't realise how difficult it could get,
Don't know how to survive.
Empty soul, wandering eyes,
Blank pages, drunken sight.
You were not the one,
But still something doesn't feel right.
I've moved on or so I think, or
Maybe what I really want to believe.
I walk past crowds, all a blur,
My vision and thoughts collide.
My heart is a constant racer,
And my mind is not far behind.
I wonder what I really need,
A hug, a smile, an assurance of things all turning out to be
fine,
A little hope or a wandering soul just like me.

30

Is it a little too late in the night?
Your images flash, though you're out of sight
I stumble upon the memories
Sometime in the morning
When I couldn't sleep
Just another day when my thoughts overpower me
I kept you close
I knew we were meant to be
Those eyes that tell me different stories each day
Have lost their way into nothingness
Those words that used to make up
For an entertaining conversation
Have been tied up in shackles of reality
Is it a little too late?
To miss you.

31

For when you feel all hopeless,
Surrounded by shattered glass.
There's a hand, always there to pull you up,
Not once, they let you think you're alone,
Not once they let you shed pools of tears.
Sometimes you drift apart,
But always find each other.
Each time you falter,
Each time you fall.
They know about all your firsts,
From your very best to your absolute worst.
Quarrels to laughter to tears,
Surviving and living together undeterred.

32

Whisper in my ear, I doubt if,
You'd be able to get across a word or two.
'Cause I have been restless for far too long,
Thinking about stuff, clouding my mind.
Decked up in an oversized sweater,
Finding solace in red-wine.
Lately I haven't been jammed,
With your texts or cruel intensions.
Many nights have passed,
Empty sheets losing your essence.
No sign of you,
I guess you've found someone else.
And now if you ever come back,
I won't ever know how to love again.
You were the first and I hoped,
The only one.
But yes I got played,
Fell head over heels.
Should have known better,
Should have looked closely,
Into those deceiving eyes!
So come by at your own risk,
And whisper in my ear.
I'm sure this time it will,
Go unheard.

33

She stood amidst a storm,

Carrying a whirlwind of emotions,

Unsure of whom to choose.

Caught between the present and the 'could be',

She watched the waves go back and forth,

Thought of how she could free flow.

The many intricacies of being in love,

Taking a toll, a rollercoaster and a never ending constant surge.

She opens her arms,

And allows the air to soothe her worries,

Allows her heart to beat for more than one.

As people spit their opinions,

She feels invincible,

No one can affect her,

Who do you love?

Whoever I choose to, she says.

34

What have you known?
If not loved and lost
Loving is but a journey of two souls
But losing is what stops you midway
Loving makes you accustomed to each other
Losing makes you value, makes you suffer
Love is what we call bittersweet
Losing, a reality check!
What have you done?
If not loved and lost
What have you done?
If never loved at all

Unearthing Layers

Don't turn your face from reality,
It's deep-rooted, agony
Scream only to get silenced
Rise, awaken and fathom.

35

A tap on the door, then two

She peeps out then creeps back in.

Panic strikes as the strangers ask her to let them in,

She locks the door and blocks possible entrances.

Crouched in a corner,

Unsure of escape.

She clings to hope,

Says a silent prayer.

Suddenly she hears footsteps,

And tries to run.

Caught by the hair,

Pinned to the ground.

Hunger for lust unleashed itself,

Humans in demonic forms appeared.

Her cries, her struggle went unheard.

Her adornments torn one by one.

Her eyes stunned, unmoved.

The tear that falls down her cheek stops midway,

Knowing its fate.

Tousled hair, not because she woke up from a good night's
sleep,

Her shame multiplies as she lays in all her nakedness.

It was not her fault.

But she is made to believe otherwise!

The demons laugh as they crave for their next prey,
For them it's all a game.
She hasn't moved from the corner they left her at,
Clinging to torn pieces of cloth which barely covered her.
She used to fear the dark once,
But it's light that she's afraid of now.
Swollen eyes have a hit a drought,
Staring into the darkness, looking for a reason to go on.

36

The old man,
With hair so grey.
A little unbalanced,
Give him some way.
Each child sat attentively,
As he had many a tales to tell.
With usual joint pains and high blood pressure,
He wasn't keeping well.
He proudly flashed his toothless smile,
Didn't care much about his poor eyesight.
He tried hiding his emptiness,
Just wanted someone to hug him tight.
Today when I happened to stop by,
I came to know the old man had died.
I don't know what came over me,
I was numb and then I cried.

37

Blackened hands, blackened face,
A crack of smile visible in that haze.
Not bothered about the world, not a penny in her pockets,
She satisfied herself with little things.
A set of toys out for sale,
Her little rag jingling with coins.
"Please buy these, I'm hungry!"
But hardly anybody would pay attention.
Scorching heat hitting her hard,
She wished for that ice-popsicle.
The break of dusk,
Her saddened soul.
She had to sleep hungry again!
Walking home, tried to brighten up,
"Have you got food for me?" her sister asked.
Convincing her sister to gulp down the water again.
At the break of dawn,
She hoped for her hopes to come true.

38

An open Letter from Earth

You chopped the roots which sun-bathed for decades,
Your long haul promises on fake premise.
I gave you ample to fulfil more than you desired,
Its value hardly mattered as your greed multiplied.

The green is seen all burnt in flames,
A deadly death, your dainty prey.
The colors I once painted with varied petals,
Search for breath and hope you are struck with the realisation.

They once feared the brunt of the axe,
Now they have grown accustomed.
Laid low and silent for quite a while,
Enough! as chaos unfurls, calamities on the rise.

What took you so long to realise?
Distraught by circumstance,
You look around, bewildered eyes.
Desperate to find an escape,
All this while I was at your place.
Introspect before it is too late,
For you lead yourself to destruction,
And the end of the human race.

39

There she stood,
All glitz and glam.
Another day, the same man,
Things have not changed,
She prepares to not break again.
"Adjust," she was taught, "be flexible!"
Girls have to do it for a happy relationship.
No, he didn't torture her,
Just some belittling remarks it were,
"Take it in jest my so called darling", he used to say.
She a constant centre of jokes that were not jokes anymore,
"You silly girl, you don't know the world, you have hardly travelled,"
"You can be good as Mommy taught, you should just agree to what I say,"
"Your identity is pointless without my name,"
"My name gives you worth."
She flashes her white teeth as he continues belittling all that she is,
Those teary eyes have given multiple excuses to not be what they are,
That face has shined through all the dust it had to face,
Those lips have moved from initial sadness to their pretentious smile in seconds.

Look at her now,
Can you make out her state?
She is unaware of freedom,
She is still adjusting,
She is being what her mother told her to be.
Their thoughts don't match,
Doesn't matter, just agree to what he says.
A new morning comes,
And she prepares to smile wide again.

Micropoetry

I may not seem like a lot of words,
But I hold deeper meanings.

40

Sobriety
Does deceive
When a chaotic inside
Displays an outward calm
Fusing and diffusing simultaneously.

41

The myriad colors
Disorient me from pretentious beauty
Caving in yet falling out.

42

Leaving
Unanswered questions
Forsaken toxicity
No remnants of you
Disintegrating.

43

Night
Hovers, shadowing
Bringing out darkness
A sight mostly hidden
Gets revealed gradually.

44

Thoughts
Swallow you
Wire the unwired
A pool of deep water
Overflowing.

45

Glory
Costing shatter
Tearful silent screeches
Showing possible wins
Gory.

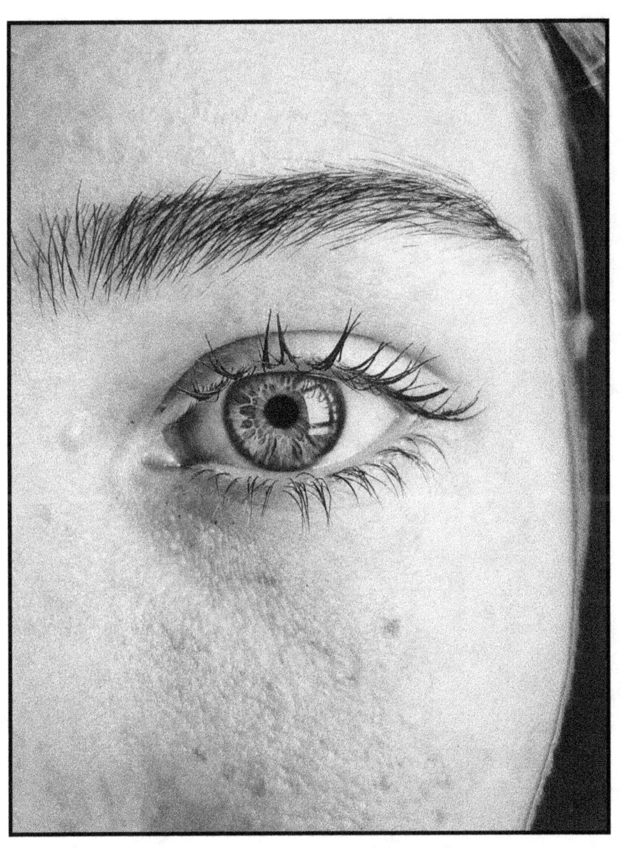

46

Bleed
Feel deeply
Take in slowly
Calm the nuances
Halt for the moments
Breathe.

47

Transcending
From battered hopes
Leaving shattered woes
Take me by the hand
Reveal.

48

Freeing my thoughts
They cage me, no escape!
Gradual burnout.

49

Walls tower her exposure
She does nothing to break away
A void needn't be filled.

50

Heart
Beating faster
I'm hardly breathing
Captivated in your embrace
Surrendering.

The woods are lovely, dark and deep,
But I have promises to keep,
And miles to go before I sleep,
And miles to go before I sleep.

\- ROBERT FROST

About the Author

Raghavi Jhanjee

Date of birth : 03rd May, 1999

Place of birth : Agra

Email		ragzzzjhanjee@gmail.com
Instagram		https://www.instagram.com/ the_regularteenager

Raghavi Jhanjee is a writer and poet. Currently, she is a student of Journalism and Mass Communication at Bennett University - A Times Group Initiative. A curious child at heart, she finds solace in her words. She has done her schooling from All Saints' College, Nainital and Delhi Public School, Agra. She is an avid reader and enjoys reading the poems of Robert Frost and Elizabeth Barrett Browning. Her favorite authors are J.K Rowling and Danielle Steel. She runs a full-fledged poetry blog on Instagram with the handle @the_regularteenager.

In the stormy night,
When she couldn't find the words to speak,
A mighty sword, companion for life,
Sought her companionship.
Pages filled with endless words,
All sprung from the depths of her soul.
On dreariest of days,
She found comfort in the pages of her diary.
Scattered pile,
Building and growing one day at a time.

Special Thanks

(names listed alphabetically)

Aakriti Mahinderu	Fraz Mallik	Pakhi Malhotra
Aditi Singhal	Gautam Rawat	Parul Singh
Aditiya Sharma	Ishaan Arora	Pooja Mehta
Aditya Misra	Japna Batra	Poonam Bhargava
Anam Aquil	Jathin Nair	Pradeep Gandhi
Anu Chopra	Jayti Upadhyay	Preeti Moondra
Anukriti Vashistha	Karan Jhanjee	Priyanka Jhanjee
Anuradha Dev	Kiara Deepak	Priyati Sharma
Apoorva Sharma	Kiran Ohri	Raj Abhisar Agarwal
Arpita Ankit	Krishan Lal Magon	Rajan Malik
Arshita Agarwal	Kriti Bansal	Rajat Oberoi
Ashok Katyal	Manoj Kumar	Rajesh Sharma
Atul Khandelwal	Medha Sharma	Rakesh Khazanchi
Ayush Chaturvedi	Mehul Tekchandani	Rama Kaushik
Chander Daultani	Mohul Ohri	Ramesh Kumar P
Deena Dayal Narayanan	Muskan Guliani	Ramesh Nair
Devanshi Narang	Nandini Nandal	Rhythm Dua
Devendra Singh Negi	Nanki Mehta	Ritu Gulati
Devesh Srivastav	Navroop Khera	Rupanshi Chitransh
Dheeraj Teegala	Nikhil Anil	Sabatini Shruthi Hussain
Diganta Debnath	Nishant Jha	Sadasivan Nair
Dinesh Sehra	Nithin Kalorth	Sahil Murshid

Sakshi Mehra

Sanjay Jhanjee

Sanjiti Mohan

Sanyukta Agarwal

Satwik Narayana Nadimpalli

Saumya Bhatt

Shajan Kumar

Simran Jha

Simran Dhillon

Shimaila Khan

Shirin Sehgal

Shiv Mahinderu

Shivam Chawla

Shivam Shukla

Shruti Khattar

Shubhrali Ben

Shweta Lamba

Siddhartha Misra

Sohom Pramanick

Somya Bhadauria

Sonal Lamba

Sonali Datt

Sumant Srivastava

Sunita Gupta

Sumita Vaid

Sweety Khattar

Tanishq Chawla

Tejaswini Mittal

Udit Juneja

Vaishnavi Gupta

Vanita Lal

Vartika Madan

Vidhanshu Kumar

Vidya Deshpande

Vikas Mahinderu

Vinay Malhotra

Vineet Verma

Vinod Shastri

Yash Mishra

EMBRACE

RAGHAVI JHANJEE

Email your questions, experiences,
and suggestions to the author at
ragzzzjhanjee@gmail.com

Your Experiences